This book belongs to :

....

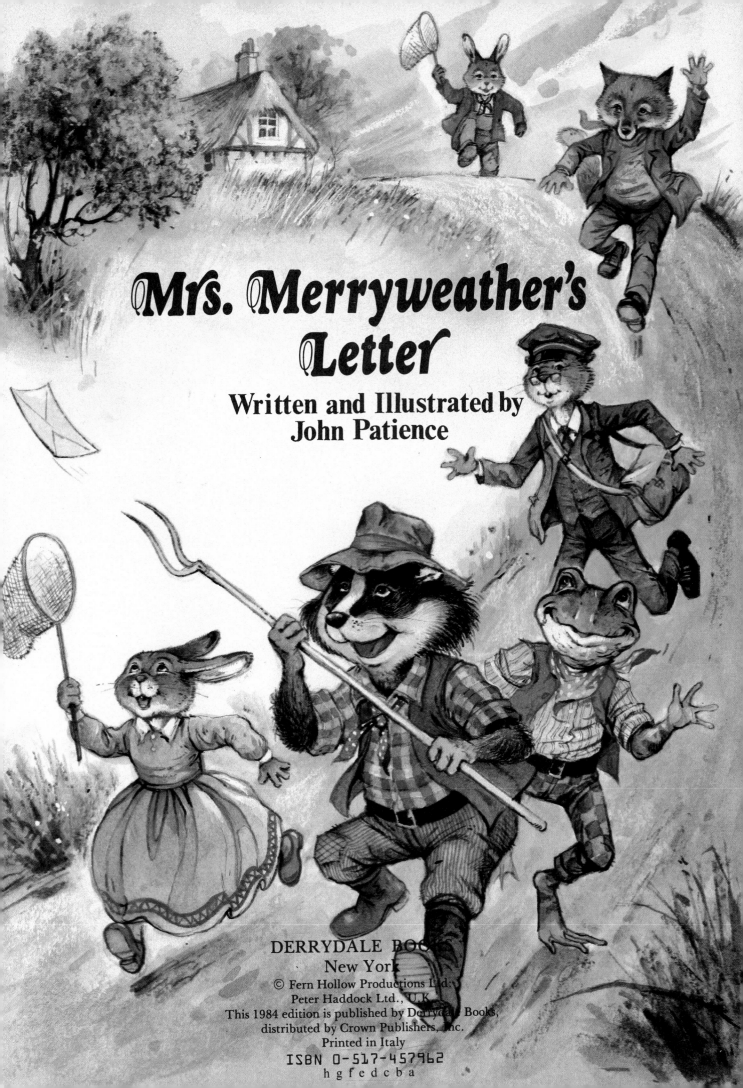

Mrs. Merryweather's Letter

Written and Illustrated by
John Patience

DERRYDALE BOOKS
New York
© Fern Hollow Productions Ltd.
Peter Haddock Ltd., U.K.
This 1984 edition is published by Derrydale Books,
distributed by Crown Publishers, Inc.
Printed in Italy
ISBN 0-517-457962
h g f e d c b a

Mrs. Merryweather, who lived in Poppletown, had just
finished writing a long letter to her friend in Fern Hollow.
She signed the letter with a flourish of her quill pen,

> Your very dear friend,

> Matilda Merryweather.

P.S. The weather here is wonderful — it is raining cats and
dogs!

Putting up her umbrella, the happy duck splashed her way along the street to the mailbox. The raindrops made little bubbles in the puddles and the oil from the traffic made rainbow patterns in the streams which ran down the gutters. Mrs. Merryweather began to sing:

"Quack, quack the rain pours down
This is the weather for me
Let it patter and pour
And drizzle galore
And a happy duck I shall be."

"Off you go," she said, popping the letter into the box, and she waddled back home again.

By the next morning Mrs. Merryweather's letter was in Mr. Periwinkle's mailbag, along with all the other letters he had to deliver. The weather in Fern Hollow was very windy, and Mr. Periwinkle was having considerable trouble in pedaling his bicycle. Suddenly, as he turned the corner by Boris Blink's bookshop, a great gust of wind caught him and

blew him over. The letters spilled out of his bag and blew
away down the street. The poor mailman hurried after
them and managed to catch all but one, and that was
Mrs. Merryweather's letter; away it sailed, high over the
rooftops.

At the watermill, Mr. Croaker was busy loading his barge with sacks of flour, which he would later take to Poppletown. The most difficult part of the job was walking along the plank from the riverbank onto the barge. This required a good sense of balance. Unfortunately Mr. Croaker completely lost his, when Mrs. Merryweather's letter blew by right under his nose. Thinking the letter might be something important, Mr. Croaker made a grab for it and the next moment he found himself in the river. Mrs. Merryweather's letter seemed to hover above him for a second and then it danced away on the wind over the tops of the trees.

Farmer Bramble emptied the bucket of swill into the pigs' trough. "Eat up," he said. Grunting with pleasure, the pigs began to gobble up the food. Just then, out of the corner of his eye, Farmer Bramble caught sight of something fluttering by. It was Mrs. Merryweather's letter. "I wonder if that's for me?" he cried. Leaping over the wall of the sty, he grabbed a pitchfork and rushed after the letter, trying to catch it on the prongs of the fork. But Farmer Bramble quickly ran out of breath and puffed his way back to the pig sty, where he found he had left the gate open and all the pigs had run away!

13

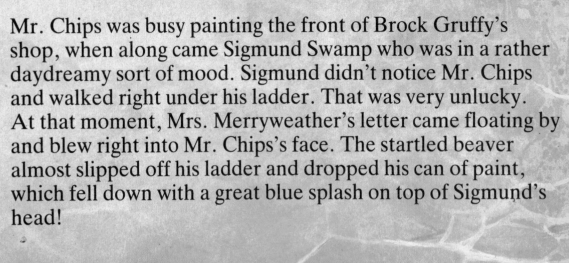

Mr. Chips was busy painting the front of Brock Gruffy's shop, when along came Sigmund Swamp who was in a rather daydreamy sort of mood. Sigmund didn't notice Mr. Chips and walked right under his ladder. That was very unlucky. At that moment, Mrs. Merryweather's letter came floating by and blew right into Mr. Chips's face. The startled beaver almost slipped off his ladder and dropped his can of paint, which fell down with a great blue splash on top of Sigmund's head!

16

All that day Mrs. Merryweather's letter blew around the
village. Lots of people tried to catch it but no one succeeded.
At last, as evening came, the wind dropped and the letter
fluttered down to rest in a bird's nest. The bird itself was fast
asleep and didn't notice the letter slip quietly in beside it.

When the bird woke up
the next morning, it was
very annoyed to see the letter
cluttering up its nest and quickly
tossed it out. Airborne again,
Mrs. Merryweather's letter went
fluttering over the railroad station
where, just then, a train was
arriving. And who should step
out of one of the carriages but
Mrs. Merryweather. The duck
didn't notice her letter flying
by, but handed her ticket to
Mr. Twinkle and waddled out of
the station.

Mrs. Willowbank was up to her elbows in soapy water as she scrubbed away at her washing. Suddenly, through the open window, in blew Mrs. Merryweather's letter.

Mrs. Willowbank picked up the letter and saw that it was
addressed to her! "It's from Matilda," she cried, reading the
letter. "She's coming to visit me this morning." As she spoke
there was a knock at the door. It was Mrs. Merryweather
herself. "I see you got my letter," she said. "Yes," replied
Mrs. Willowbank. "It arrived by airmail!"
Soon the two friends were sharing a pot of tea and a lovely
plum cake and wondering how on earth the letter had
managed to deliver itself without any help from the mailman!

Fern Hollow

MR CHIPS'S HOUSE

MR WILLOWBANK'S
COBBLERS SHOP

MR CROAKER'S WATERMILL

STRIPEY'S HOUSE

SCHOOL

THE JOLLY VOLE
HOTEL

RIVER FERNY

MR ACORN'S
BAKERY

MR RUSTY'S HOUSE

POST OFFICE

BORIS BLINKS'S
BOOKSHOP

MR PRICKLES'S HOUSE

MR TWINKLE'S
HOUSE

MR TUTTLEEBEE'S
SHOP

MR THIMBLE'S
TAILORS SHOP

WINDYWOOD